Just Desserts

Also by Hallie Durand
Dessert First

Just Desserts

by Hallie Durand
with illustrations
by Christine Davenier

atheneum books for young readers

NEW YORK   LONDON   TORONTO   SYDNEY

ATHENEUM BOOKS FOR YOUNG READERS
An imprint of Simon & Schuster Children's Publishing Division
1230 Avenue of the Americas, New York, New York 10020
This book is a work of fiction. Any references to historical events, real
people, or real locales are used fictitiously. Other names, characters,
places, and incidents are products of the author's imagination, and
any resemblance to actual events or locales or persons, living or dead,
is entirely coincidental.

ATHENEUM BOOKS FOR YOUNG READERS is a registered trademark of
Simon & Schuster, Inc.
For information about special discounts for bulk purchases, please
contact Simon & Schuster Special Sales at 1-866-506-1949 or
business@simonandschuster.com.
The Simon & Schuster Speakers Bureau can bring authors to your
live event. For more information or to book an event, contact the
Simon & Schuster Speakers Bureau at 1-866-248-3049 or visit our
website at www.simonspeakers.com.
Book design by Ann Bobco
The text for this book is set in Adobe Garamond Pro.
The illustrations for this book are rendered in pen and ink washes.
Manufactured in the United States of America
0610 MTN
First Edition
10 9 8 7 6 5 4 3 2 1
Library of Congress Cataloging-in-Publication Data
Durand, Hallie.
Just Desserts / Hallie Durand ; illustrated by
Christine Davenier. — 1st ed.
p. cm.
Summary: Third-grader Dessert, inspired by Mrs. Howdy Doody's
lessons about the American Revolution, decides she and her friends
should fight back against annoying siblings, but the club she starts
only makes matters worse.
ISBN 978-1-4169-6387-5
[1. Brothers and sisters—Fiction. 2. Clubs—Fiction. 3. Schools—
Fiction. 4. Restaurants—Fiction. 5. Family life—Fiction.] I. Davenier,
Christine, ill. II. Title.
PZ7.D9313Jus 2010
[Fic]—dc22
2009018400

For Charlotte Reine Steiner, who first said,
"Annoying siblings."

CHAPTER ONE
FISHING

Mummy always says that you never know what's going to happen from one moment to the next, but I think she's kookaloosa. I guess that's because every single day of my life is pretty much the same. My alarm clock buzzes at 7:10 a.m., which is just about the time Wolfie and Mushy start rattling their cribs. Wolfie is two and Mushy is one, and we call them the Beasties (that should tell you just about everything you need to know about them). After I get dressed and eat breakfast, I'm supposed to help my four-year-old sister, Charlie, get up, and it's impossible to pull her blankets down one at a time, exactly evenly, the way she likes. So she always starts screaming, and then I cover my ears, and as soon as I do, she starts clawing me. That's the bad part about Charlie. The good part about her is that she'll do whatever I want her to for a little teensy-weensy piece of gum (I store it in my jewelry box). The bus comes at 7:40, and I always let my dog Chunky out into the yard when I leave. I sit with Sharon S. and Bonnie A., behind Evan C. And when we get to school, we usually walk to Mrs. Howdy Doody's room together. She's our third-grade teacher, and I'll probably never know if that's her God-given name or not. Even lunchtime is the same every day.

Today was no different. At 11:50 Mrs. Howdy Doody said to line up, so I picked up my lunch box and I stood between Billy and Donnie. (They are twins and I've known them forever.)

Mrs. Howdy Doody opened the door, and I could smell the hot lunch in the air. I tilted my head up and sniffed to get more of the smell inside my nose. The hot lunch *always* smelled delicious. But then I tilted my head back down because today, just like every other day, I was not allowed to buy that hot lunch. My dad says I sound like a broken record every time I ask for it, but I think *he* does when he says the same thing back each

time: "We're a food family, Dessert. I treat my staff like family and my family like staff." What he really means is that we own a restaurant called Fondue Paris, and he always makes some kind of meal for the staff to eat before they start working their shifts. I get the leftovers in my Thermos. And what that really means is that I don't ever get anything good for lunch.

When we got to the cafeteria, I sat down at my table with Sharon, Evan, Bonnie, Billy, Donnie, and Emily V. My lunch box smelled like 409, as usual, the same cleaning stuff my parents spray the counters with at home. It seemed just plain wrong—the hot lunch in the air smelled so good, and my lunch box smelled so bad. But I was hungry, and I didn't have anything else, so I unzipped it and opened it up. And there was that ugly metal Thermos staring up at me, just like it did every other day. Crud.

I unscrewed the lid and took a look

inside. I didn't like what I saw—orange-colored noodles with some little green things and clumps of mystery meat. I call it mystery meat because it's crunchy and chewy and it's not a fruit or vegetable. I stuck my fork in there and pulled out one of the crunchy-chewy clumps—for all I knew it was pigeon.

Evan saw the gook on my fork and said, "That looks like earwax."

"It's crunchier than earwax," I said. "Want to try it?"

I wasn't surprised when Evan said, "I only try things I recognize."

I twirled my fork a few times and said,

"Another day, another skunk meal."

"I see why you call it that," said Emily. "It *always* smells bad."

I put my fork back in and plugged my nose with my free hand. But this time I pulled out a rind of smelly white cheese. (It looked like that rubber stuff on the bottom of my sneakers.)

I took my hand off my nose so I could touch it, and it felt like rubber too. And that's when I decided that putting my fork in that Thermos of leftover staff meal was like going fishing at the town dump. But at least it was a Friday, and I didn't have to "fish" on weekends.

CHAPTER TWO
THE BANK

After school, when I went up to my room, I nearly tripped over Charlie, who was sitting on the landing at the top of the stairs with a big pile of money.

"Is that my money?" I asked.

"No," she said. "It's mine. Mummy says saving money is healthy for my toolbox."

"You don't have a toolbox," I said.

"Yes I do," Charlie replied, making swirly patterns with her pennies. "You just can't see it."

That was true. I didn't see anything

toolbox-ish at all. "Then where is it?"

"Right in here," said Charlie, pointing to her head. "It's imaginary." I had heard of imaginary friends before, but not imaginary toolboxes.

"What's it for?" I asked.

"It's a magic place to keep good habits. Mummy told me about it," she answered proudly.

Now I was beginning to understand. Mummy must have invented the toolbox to get Charlie to be good. And Charlie had fallen for it. "I already put three things in there," Charlie continued. "Washing my hands, saying thank you, and brushing my hair."

This could be interesting. I kind of liked the idea of Charlie behaving like a civilized

9

human being. . . . Maybe this "toolbox" would come in handy. I started to make a mental list of all the things I could put in that magic box for her: *fold Dessert's clothes, make Dessert's bed, straighten Dessert's closet, sharpen Dessert's pencils, keep the Beasties out of Dessert's room* . . . But before I could even tell Charlie how I like my pencils sharpened (not too pointy), Mummy came upstairs and told me to leave my shoes on because we were going to the bank. She said that we were each going to open a savings account.

"I don't need a savings account," I said. "Panda saves my money for me."

"Well, Panda's going to learn about savings too then," said Mummy. "Bring him along." Sometimes what seems promising is not promising at all. That "magic place to keep good habits" was turning out to be an enemy in disguise. I did not want to take Panda to the bank.

But less than two minutes later, I was sitting in the mini-van, and Mummy was backing out of our driveway. I didn't want Panda to get worried, so I held him in my lap, facedown. I even kept his eyes against my shirt when we walked inside. "Get four deposit slips, Dessert," said Mummy. "And meet us at the coin counter in the back."

I handed Panda to Mummy and said, "Make sure you keep his eyes covered."

When I came back with the deposit slips, Charlie had already run her money through the machine. She had twenty-three dollars and seventeen cents. Then Mummy put Panda in my arms. I looked him in the eyes, and he looked back at me. I felt like he knew what I was about to do. "I have no choice," I whispered to him. "And it's all her fault." I pointed with my thumb at Charlie, who was standing behind me.

"There are people in line, Dessert," said Mummy, which meant that I couldn't stand there forever.

Sometimes it's easier to do something you don't want to do if you do it really fast. So I turned Panda upside down and pulled the plug out of his head.

I couldn't even think about how he felt as I watched his brains come out—all those quarters, dimes, nickels, and pennies pouring out of my precious Panda. There were even some gold one-dollar coins. Why hadn't I thought of taking out the gold one-dollar coins? The machine would probably just think they were old yellowed quarters. I looked at my poor empty Panda and thought about all my money. All the money I had saved over the years. I had earned it for report cards. I had earned it for working at Fondue. I had even earned it for helping Billy and Donnie's mom with a garage sale. And Dad had paid me a dollar to find his sunglasses one time. Now here I was, standing before the coin counter with Panda's plug in my hand, saying good-bye to my personal money supply, saying good-bye to my entire life savings—and it was all because of Charlie.

My total was one hundred thirty-six dollars and ninety-three cents. Every single one of those beautiful coins had disappeared. I had walked into the bank with my heavy, clinking, clanking Panda in my arms. My *happy*, heavy, clinking, clanking Panda. And now I was walking out with a silent, brokenhearted Panda—a silent, brokenhearted Panda whose brains had been dumped out of his head with no warning whatsoever. My Panda did not clink or clank anymore . . . and all I had to show for it was a small piece of white paper that said "Receipt."

CHAPTER THREE

THE GARBAGE CAN

When I woke up on Monday morning, Panda was still staring at me with his big black eyes, just like he'd done all weekend. I was convinced that he blamed me for his condition, even though it was all Charlie's fault. It seemed to me that there were really only bad surprises in life. When Mummy says you never know what's going to happen from one moment to the next, she is forgetting the most important word. BAD. She *should* say you never know what BAD thing is going to

happen from one moment to the next. Before
I went downstairs, I put Panda by the window
so he could look outside, and when I sat down
on the bus, I waved good-bye to him.

"I'm bankrupt," I said to Sharon. "Thanks
to Charlie and her toolbox."

"What toolbox?"
said Sharon. So I
told her about
Charlie's "magic
place to keep
good habits" and
how it had really
been invented to mess up my life.

"That sounds awful," said Sharon.

"It is awful," I said.

The rest of the morning went by like it always does, and when we got to the cafeteria, I opened up my lunch box, and there was that stinkin' Thermos again. I was the only one at our whole table who got a Thermos every single day. The next thing I knew was that I heard the voice of Amy D., the meanest girl in our school, the one who stuffed leaves in my mouth in first grade and called me "Tree."

"Dessert's eating garbage!" she hollered from the other table. "That Thermos looks like a miniature garbage can."

And that made me so mad I wanted to throw my lunch box at her. Because Amy D., the awful, nosy Amy D., was right. My Thermos *did* look like a miniature garbage can: It was metal and it smelled bad and it had a lid. Plus it was full of garbage.

Somehow Bonnie knew I couldn't put my fork back in there after what Amy said and she handed me four pretzel sticks. "That's all I have," she said. "My sister took the last bag of Doritos."

Even though I like pretzel knots more than pretzel sticks, and I like Doritos more than either of those, today I was happy to get any junk food at all. "Thanks, Bonnie," I said. Emily passed along one gumdrop. (She is never generous with her food.)

Donnie said, "Take what you like," and Billy gave me half of his granola bar. Evan handed over three Sun Chips and Sharon gave me a piece of a rice cake.

And even though my friends were kind to me, life seemed unfair. Everybody else had food they liked for lunch. And all I had was a miniature garbage can and a few donations from people who felt sorry for me.

CHAPTER FOUR

IT'S NOT FINE

The next morning Dad was packing my lunch when I got downstairs.

"Am I ever going to get to buy hot lunch?" I asked.

"You know I don't endorse that, Dessert. Not when we have a Thermosful of fine food sitting right here."

Sometimes I feel like Dad would say our food was fine even if it was full of hair. "It's not fine, Dad."

"Guston calls it 'divine,'" Dad replied. I

know why Guston calls it that. Because he's our head waiter, and head waiters have to be polite.

Just then Charlie walked in. I couldn't believe she had gotten up without squawking. Mummy must have told her that was good for her toolbox. "I bet Charlie doesn't think it's divine," I said to Dad. I knew she would take my side because I looked right at her and made a chewing noise. (That's my secret signal for giving her gum.)

Daddy gave a forkful to Charlie, and she ate it and said, "Mmm-mmmmmmm!" Then she held up her fork and said, "May I have some more?"

I made a louder chewing noise in Charlie's ear, because I thought she must not have gotten the message. But Charlie said, "Stop it, Dessert." Then she licked her lips, looked at Dad again, and said, "It's so healthy for my toolbox!"

"Garbage is not healthy for your toolbox," I said to Charlie, and as soon as I said it I knew I was in trouble. The words had popped out right in front of Dad.

"Did you call my food garbage?" he said.

"I didn't mean to," I said. "I'm sorry."

"Get dressed," he said.

When I got to my room, I stood in front of my closet, staring at my clothes. I didn't feel like getting dressed. Was it really only yesterday

23

that Charlie worked for me? Was it only yesterday that girls stuck together? Was it only yesterday that I made the rules? As I sat there, even though the sun was shining through my window, my room seemed gloomy. I was on my own. And it was all because of Charlie's toolbox. The only one I could really count on was Chunky. You'd never guess he's forty-nine in dog years (he looks good). "It's over," I whispered to him. "I'm not the leader anymore." And he looked at me with his wise eyes, and I knew he wished he could fix it. But there are some things even Chunky can't do.

I was four when Charlie came along. I thought she was an alien for a long time because she

didn't speak English. She only used hand signals.

But then Mummy showed me her belly button and told me that it proved she's a member of the human race. I knew Mummy was telling the truth, but it still doesn't really make sense. How can I, Donahue Penelope Schneider, also known as Dessert, belong to the same species as Charlene Josephine Schneider? I guess you can't rely on science alone, because Charlie

IS ANNOYING,

CAN'T STOP TALKING

ABOUT HER TOOLBOX,

IS NOT AS SMART AS ME BUT

CAN'T BE BRIBED

ANYMORE,

SAYS SHE LIKES THE STUFF IN

MY THERMOS,

&

THANKS TO HER I WILL BE STUCK

EATING GARBAGE

FOREVER.

CHAPTER FIVE

MY PLATE WAS EMPTY

That evening I was hoping that Dad had forgotten about the word I called his food. And when he yelled, "COME AND GET IT!" at suppertime, I was relieved because it meant things might be back to normal. I crossed my fingers and went downstairs. But I saw that Daddy had not forgotten. There on the table were six little plates. Each plate had a lemon square sitting in the middle. Except for one. The one in front of my chair.

MY
PLATE
WAS
EMPTY.

Charlie was to blame for this. She was the entire reason that the *G* word got out in front of Dad. It seemed to me that nobody even remembered that I'm the one who convinced Mummy to let us have dessert before our supper in the first place. Nobody remembered because they were too busy eating one bite after another of that buttery, powdery sugary crust with that bright lemony layer on top. That bright lemony layer that wakes you up when it reaches your mouth. Lemon squares are better than lemon-meringue pie because the bottom layer is so much softer than pie crust. I had to sit right there in my chair watching my rotten sister take one bite after another of her square. I felt like I could see inside her mouth as the sour-sweet surprise went from front to back, like a delicious wave. Nobody even seemed to care that when I looked down at my plate,

all I saw was my own face staring back up at me.

"I'm sorry I called it garbage, Daddy," I said, with my eyes fixed on Charlie. I was hoping I'd get a lemon square. Charlie was looking right back at me, with her fork in her mouth.

"Apology accepted," said Dad.

"May I have a lemon square?"

"No dessert tonight," Dad said.

This was not right. All I did was share my feelings about my Thermos, and now they had taken away the one thing I look forward to all day. Dessert. The very thing I was named after.

Let me explain. When I was born, my Grandma Reine (who was French) said, *"Mon dessert est servi."* That means, "My dessert is served." Ever since, I've been known as Dessert, and I usually sign my name like this:

"Please clear the plates," Mummy said to me.

But Charlie hopped up and said, "I'll do it!"

And that made me feel even worse. Charlie wasn't clearing the plates for me tonight. She was clearing the plates for her toolbox, which is what got me in trouble to begin with. At that moment, it all became very clear to me: Annoying Charlie and her annoying toolbox were going to decrease my life expectancy. I would probably die before the age of nine.

CHAPTER SIX

GENERAL HOWDY DOODY

The next morning I said to my teacher, "Good morning, Mrs. Howdy Doody," like I usually do, but she did not say, "Good morning, Dessert Schneider," like she usually does. Instead she said, "Dessert Schneider, it's best to make eye contact when you greet someone." So I looked up and saw that she had on a white wig and a weird black hat.

She swept off her hat and pointed her leg out at me.

"Welcome to our study of the American

Revolution!" she said. "You may call me General Howdy Doody, and you may curtsy. That's
the colonial way." (I went ahead and curtsied
to Mrs. Howdy Doody, because it seemed like
the only way I was going to get to my desk.)
Once we were all seated, she started marching
around the room,
saying, "The colo-
nists marched to

their own drummers. Stand up, ye colonists, and show your appreciation for George Washington and the Continental Army."

When we all stood up, Mrs. Howdy Doody said, "I cherish my freedom because I can think, feel, and do as I please. . . . Why, just this morning I thought about colonial times, and that made me start to feel independent, so I dressed as I pleased! And now it's your turn. Tell me about freedom, my dear happy learners. Tell me what it means to you."

Emily put her hand up first, and Mrs. Howdy Doody called on her. "I am free to wear a ponytail every day," said Emily. "Except when we have company and my mother does my hair."

"Good thinking," said Mrs. Howdy Doody. "Billy, please contribute."

"I'm free to pretend I'm Donnie," said Billy. "Even when Donnie doesn't want me to!"

"Very nice, Donnie—um, I mean Billy," said Mrs. Howdy Doody.

Donnie started to put his hand down, but Mrs. Howdy Doody called on him anyway. "Donnie, don't let shyness get the better of you," she said. "Talk to me."

Donnie said, "I wanted to say what Billy said except with the word Billy, not Donnie."

"And you are free to do so," said Mrs. Howdy Doody. "Your turn, Amy D."

"I am free to choose my own friends," said Amy D., looking around the room.

"I can't argue with that," said Mrs. Howdy Doody.

And after everybody but me had shared, Mrs. Howdy Doody said, "You are free to keep your thoughts to yourself, Dessert. But we would like to hear them, if you are so inclined."

I knew what this meant. It meant I was not really free to keep my thoughts to myself. It meant that everybody was watching me, waiting for me to say something. But I couldn't think of anything to say because I didn't feel free at all, so I looked at her and said softly, "I'm not inclined."

"And that's what freedom is really all about," said Mrs. Howdy Doody. "We can do what we want to do when we want to do it! And what do you know? It's 11:11, my dear happy learners. Make a wish!"

I made two wishes: for Charlie to go back to her old self and for me to get hot lunch. I guess I do have a little bit of freedom, just like Mrs. Howdy Doody said. I have the freedom to make wishes.

CHAPTER SEVEN

GUNG

Mummy was on the phone when I got home and Dad was at work, so I put my lunch box on the counter and went upstairs. But when I walked into my room, Charlie was waiting for me. She looked at me and said, "Messy rooms are not—"

"Get out," I said.

"But messy—"

"Get out of my room or I'll call the police," I said.

She must have thought calling the police

would be bad for her toolbox, because she went downstairs. And since I couldn't bribe her with gum anymore, I decided to go ahead and chew it myself. But when I opened the top right drawer of my jewelry box, there was no gum in there. All my gum, every teeny tiny scrap I'd saved, was gone.

"Chaaarrrrrrrrlieeeeeeeeeee!" I yelled. "Chaaarrrrrrrrlieeeeeeee-eeeeeeeeeeeeeeee!"

She didn't come up, so I yelled louder. "CHAAAAAAAAAARR-LIEEEEEEEEEEEE!"

But Charlie didn't appear. Wolfie did instead, with Mushy at his side. (They always travel together.)

"Is your name Charlie?" I said to them both.

Mushy said, "Gung."

"Gum? Do you mean you took my gum?"

"Gung," he said again, and pointed to Wolfie.

And I knew Mushy was trying to tell me that Wolfie stole my gum, because:

1. Wolfie can't be trusted.
2. Wolfie was not defending himself.
3. Wolfie smelled minty.
4. My wastebasket was upside down.

40

And that's when I realized that you don't need a toolbox to be annoying. Wolfie had used my wastebasket to get my gum. And I couldn't even tell on him, because Mummy didn't know about the gum in the first place. So I pulled Wolfie into

his room by his belt loops and nudged Mushy along with my foot. Mummy would find them soon enough, and I had homework to do.

CHAPTER EIGHT

HEAPS OF MONEY

It looked to me like my first American Revolution homework was a thinking assignment. There was a sheet of paper that said:

Ye Colonists,

On the back of this sheet you'll find

a phrase that originated

with the birth of our country and the

birth of our freedoms.

This is your talking point for our

Town Talk gathering tomorrow.

Talk to your neighbors,

talk to your parents,

talk, talk, talk about your phrase . . .

and then we'll talk to each other!

Yours in democracy,

General H. Doody

I didn't really see myself as "ye colonist," but I did turn the paper over. It said:

CONGRESS SHALL HAVE POWER TO COLLECT TAXES

I had never heard of a talking point, but I figured it meant that when Mrs. Howdy Doody pointed at me I was supposed to talk. And I didn't know much about taxes, but I liked the idea that Congress could collect them. (I've been collecting china dogs since I was three.) Best of all, there was no writing to do with this homework, so I went downstairs to work on Chunky's high five with him. My babysitter Pam says he's too old and too big to do a high five, but I don't think so.

"Don't let me forget

to sign your homework," Mummy said to me at supper.

"It was only a talking assignment," I said. "I'm supposed to talk to you about taxes."

"Oh, dear," said Mummy. "Taxes? Do you even know what they are?"

"Not really," I said. "But my sheet says that Congress has power to collect them."

"Okay," Mummy said. "You know the money we put into the offering plate at church when we go? Did you ever see Dad or me do that?" I had seen that plate plenty of times. I think I might have even dreamed about that plate.

"Yes," I said. "It's the most money I've ever seen."

"Well, that money is used to help the church," said Mummy. "And taxes are really just like that plate of money, except that every single working person in America pays them, and then people like the president use the money to help our country." I had no idea everybody sent money to the president. There was no way it would fit on a giant plate. So I said to Mummy, "Where does he keep it all, Mummy?"

"In a bank, honey, just like you keep yours." (I couldn't believe the president fell for the savings trick too.)

47

"It must be nice to collect taxes," I said. I could hardly imagine how much money the president must have. He must have the biggest bank account in the world. I didn't know how he carried all that money to the bank, but I was pretty sure it wasn't the same way I did.

CHAPTER NINE

WELCOME TO TOWN TALK

The next morning I made eye contact with Mrs. Howdy Doody, and I saw that she was still wearing the hat and wig, so I curtsied and said, "Good morning, General Howdy Doody."

"Good morning, Colonist Schneider!" she said. (She did the hat and leg thing again.)

I went to my desk, but as soon as I sat down I had to stand right back up because Mrs. Howdy Doody said, "Form a circle, ye colonists!" As we started to make a circle, she said, "Welcome to Town Talk. Here is how it works: One of you will speak, then I'll respond, and the person who spoke can choose the next speaker. Let's start with Sharon S." I counted twenty-one of us in the circle, so it didn't look like this meeting would be over anytime soon.

"I asked my parents what domestic tranquility means, and they said it means don't fight with your brothers and they won't fight with you," said Sharon. (I think her parents lied to her.)

"That sounds tranquil to me," said Mrs. Howdy Doody. "It might even work!" Then Sharon picked Billy.

"Mine said 'cruel and unusual punishment shall not be inflicted,'" said Billy.

"And how do you interpret that?"

"I told my mom spinach is cruel and unusual, but she says it's neither."

"I think she's right about that," said Mrs. Howdy Doody.

Billy said, "I choose Donnie."

"I got 'people can bear arms,'" said Donnie. "That's why I'm wearing this shirt."

"But what does that mean to you?" said Mrs. Howdy Doody.

"My dad says we have a right to protect ourselves," he said. I liked the sound of that, but I knew from experience it's not always possible.

"Thanks, Donnie," said Mrs. Howdy Doody. Then Donnie picked Evan, who told us he got "All men are created equal."

"That's part of the Declaration of Independence!" said Mrs. Howdy Doody. "What does it mean to you?"

"My dad said it means all people are entitled to life, liberty, and the pursuit of happiness," Evan said. "And I checked with my mom, and he's right."

"You know a lot!" said Mrs. Howdy Doody. "Whom do you choose?"

Evan picked me, so I said, "My phrase is 'Congress shall have power to collect taxes.' And it means that everybody pays the president, and he puts his heaps of money in the bank."

"That's the right idea," said Mrs. Howdy Doody, "but then he takes it out to pay for programs that help us. Some of them even help our school."

My mother hadn't told me the school part, but I was sick of talking, so I just said, "I choose Emily."

"Mine is, 'No taxation without representation,'" she said.

"Go on," said Mrs. Howdy Doody.

"My mom says it means that if you pay you have a say."

"I think the colonists would agree with your mom," said Mrs. Howdy Doody. "They didn't want to pay taxes to the mother country without getting something in return."

"I pick Bonnie," said Emily.

"You have to be thirty-five years old and a citizen of the United States to be president," said Bonnie, "and that means no kids can run."

"Well, not till they're grown up," Mrs. Howdy Doody said.

Bonnie picked Melissa, and Melissa picked Geezy Lou, and Geezy Lou picked

Lois, and one by one every single "colonist" shared. Amy D. was last, and by the time she finished talking about freedom of speech I felt like I'd grown roots.

"What a wonderful morning of Town Talk," said Mrs. Howdy Doody. "Now let's move on to General Howdy Doody's Minuteman Math!" (I'd never heard of Minuteman Math, but I thought I would survive it, because it sounded like it would be over in a minute.)

CHAPTER TEN

ANOTHER FAMILY NIGHT

When Mummy opened the door for me after school, she was holding our tub of crayons. That usually means it's going to be another family night at Fondue, but she hadn't mentioned it, so I said, "Are we going to Fondue?"

"Not by choice," said Mummy. "The new waiter is still in training. If it's slow, your father will join us."

I couldn't wait to get my homework done, because I'd be taking the "flight" in a little while. When you order the Fondue Flight at our restaurant (we *always* do), you begin with cheese fondue cooked right at your table, and you end with a trip to the Eiffel Tower. The tower is taller than Daddy, with red, white, and blue twinkling lights. There's a giant silver pot in the middle of it, and each day it's full of a different kind of mouth-watering dessert fondue. The fondue goes up a tube from the silver pot to the top of the tower, and when you take your "flight," you get to fill up your bowl as the fondue streams back down through the middle. Dad always says the tower makes Fondue Paris a local destination, and I think he's right. It seems like almost everybody from my school has been there.

We left in the late afternoon so that Mummy could spend more time with the new waiter. As soon as we arrived, I grabbed a menu so I could read the little sheet inside that told me today's tower flavor. It was Magic Midnight, and if I remembered correctly, Magic Midnight is very, very dark chocolate. It's as chocolaty as a glass of chocolate milk with no milk in it, only syrup. At Fondue Paris, we never get dessert until after our cheese fondue, but

Fondue Paris
TAKE YOUR FLIGHT TONIGHT

the trip to the tower is worth the wait. I saw Guston in the back and he smiled at me, but he wasn't our waiter tonight. Instead we had to have Gaby, the one Mummy was training—it was her second day.

"Our table is Number Twelve," said Mummy, and Gaby led us there. Mummy thanked Gaby and asked her to tell us about tonight's flight.

Gaby held her hands together, leaned in toward us, and said, "The flight tonight takes off with a deluxe cheese fondue for four and lands with a magic night of—um—I mean—"

"Magic Midnight!" I said. Gaby looked relieved.

"Just jot down the name on the back of

your pad so you'll remember it," Mummy said. I saw Gaby's hands shaking a little as she got her pad out from her apron pocket.

I think she scribbled "Magic Midnight" on the back of her pad, and then she said, "Now, what kind of cheese would you like? We offer Gruyère, aged Swiss, and . . . um—"

"My cheese better be cheddar!" I said loudly. Mummy frowned at me, but before she could say anything, Dad came out from the kitchen, ruffled my hair, and said, "Good day?"

"Medium," I said, because I hadn't liked standing on my feet during Amy D.'s speech but I did like the sound of Magic Midnight Fondue.

Before Daddy could say anything else, we were all surprised to see Guston jogging past our table. I've never seen him jog before.

He opened the door, and a whole bunch of grown-ups walked in.

"So much for our family meal," said Dad. "I forgot about the Newcomers Club."

Guston pushed two tables together right near the fountain, and all the grown-ups sat down. They each had a name sticker. I squinted my eyes to try to read their names— I think the one I was looking at said FORD. That seemed like a weird name, but he looked nice enough. I was wondering what other names I might see, but Mummy told me to stop staring.

"I just wanted to read their stickers," I said. "Why are they wearing them?"

"If you stop gawking, I'll tell you," she

whispered. "Most of them are new in town and they want to make friends. That's why they're in the club."

Gaby came back, put a silver fondue pot on top of a skinny metal frame, and lit the Sterno (it looks like a little can of tuna with blue Jell-O in it). She threw some garlic into the pot and started stirring. Then she added some mustard. She picked up the plate of shredded cheese next, but Mummy pushed her wrist back down. "The wine is next," said Mummy. Gaby added the wine and then picked up the plate of cheese again and sprinkled it in. Usually I get to put the cheese in, but not tonight.

"You're doing well, Gaby," said Mummy. "Just keep scraping the sides with your spoon."

Gaby smiled at me, and I said, "May I be your critic? Guston always lets me." She looked confused, so I said, "I'll see how it is." I took my skewer (it looks like a mini back-scratcher) and put a piece of bread on the end. Then I dunked it in the fondue and twirled until my skewer couldn't hold any more. I got the whole thing in my mouth while Mummy was picking up Wolfie's napkin.

Gaby was looking at me like she wanted me to hurry up, so I nodded and made an "okay" sign with my hand. Guston came by and said, "She approves, Gaby. Now we'll attend to the Newcomers." He practically pulled her away, and I saw that one of the Newcomers was waving an empty bread basket in the air. Mummy says that even though that means the waiter is too slow, nobody should ask for more bread that way. She calls it "animal behavior."

We dipped our bread and our pickles and our fingerling potatoes into the big melty pot of fondue. I love the fingerling potatoes, because they look like fat little fingers. When we were all pretty full, but not all-the-way full, it was my favorite part of the meal: It was time to take our trip to the tower. Charlie said, "I'm first," and ran up to the gleaming dark stream of Magic Midnight Fondue. When her bowl was nearly filled, I said, "My turn." But she wouldn't move.

"Acting like a hog is not good for your toolbox," I said, pushing her out of the way. At least that got her to move so I could get to the stream. I filled my bowl to the top. The fondue was dark and chocolaty and almost as shiny as a limousine. I wanted to dig right in when we got back to the table, but I remembered to say, "May I bring you some, Mummy?"

Mummy said yes, and asked me to bring a bowl for the Beasties, too, and I said, "With pleasure." (I was hoping they would need "help" finishing theirs.)

I filled two more bowls as high as I could and presented them to Mummy just as Gaby brought us a big platter of pineapple hearts, pinwheel cookies, and mandarin orange slices. Then she presented me with a small bowl of ridged chips. I hadn't told Gaby that ridged potato chips were my favorite thing to dip in chocolate fondue. "Did Dom tell you I liked chips and chocolate?" I asked.

"If that's the pastry chef's name," Gaby replied, "all she told me was to give you that bowl."

"Well, she's my friend Dom," I said. "Don't worry. She's a little grumpy till you get to know her."

Just then one of the Newcomers started waving his bread basket again.

"I'll remember that," said Gaby. "Now I'd better get some more bread." She smiled at me, but just as I was smiling back I noticed that Gaby's smile stopped and turned into a big open mouth. And the next thing I saw was my plate, my platter, and my bowl of ridged chips sailing off the side of the table. Mushy was pulling on the tablecloth, and my Magic Midnight Fondue was on the floor. Mummy got up to take him out of his high chair, but he didn't stop pulling, and then the whole tablecloth went clattering on the floor. The shiny dark fondue looked like an oil spill. There were little pools of shimmering satin with mini rivers coming out the sides.

Gaby got down on her knees and started wiping the floor with napkins. Her hands were

covered with chocolate, and she had some on her apron, too. I think I even saw some in her hair. Mummy set down Mushy and told me to watch him—but before I could stop him, Wolfie plopped right down in one of the mini chocolate pools and Mushy plopped on top of him, and they started finger-painting.

Guston came running over with Nick, a busser, who was carrying a giant mop. (I wish we had a busser at home, because they clean up everything.) Guston told Gaby to get herself a new apron. Then he said, "Mrs. Schneider, it's dangerous for the children." (That was Guston's way of telling Mummy to take them away.) Mummy led them to the door.

"Dessert," Guston said to me, "please

fetch the Newcomers some more bread." He gave me a little push toward the kitchen, and when I got there Dom stuck three baskets of bread in my hands and said, "This will keep them quiet." I delivered them to the one named Ford, and he said thanks.

"Piece o' cake," I said. My parents have told me to pretend the customer is always right since the day I arrived on Earth.

I brought the empty bread baskets back to the kitchen, where Gaby was still trying to get her apron bow even. "I can do that for you," I said, and took her apron and straightened it out. Then I wrapped it around her and said, "Right over left, left over right" as I made a smooth bow. Gaby looked like a brand-new present from the back.

"Thank you," Gaby said softly.

"Your mother's waiting for you, Dessert," Dad said.

"But I didn't get any—"

"It's been a rough night, Dessert. For everyone. You're going home." And I knew from his voice that I *was* going home. I was going home without my dessert.

And I'll never forget how wrong that felt. It was at that exact moment that I understood that sometimes the only reward for being nice is cruel and unusual punishment. I had patiently waited through our whole meal to get the Magic Midnight Fondue. I had asked Mummy if she wanted some before I sat down to eat my own. I had been nice to the Newcomers, who waved their baskets in the air like "animals," and I had helped Gaby tie her apron.

Sitting in the wayback was worse than ever tonight. There was an annoying sibling everywhere I turned. I was surrounded. Worse yet, I was beginning to think that my siblings were not just annoying. I was beginning to think they were infected with a disease of annoyingness, which had now spread to Mushy. He and he alone was responsible for what happened. And I did not get one single ridged chip dipped in Magic Midnight Fondue because of it.

CHAPTER ELEVEN

TOOTHPASTE AND KLEENEX

There weren't any cribs rattling the next morning, and my alarm had not gone off. It was already 7:25. I started to get out of bed, and then I stopped. There was something in my room I'd never seen before. And that something was pink stuff, and it was all over Wolfie's face. There was a blanket of Kleenex on my floor too, and Wolfie was sitting in the middle of it all, wiping.

"What do you think you're doing?" I asked. "And how did you get out of your crib?"

"I climb," said Wolfie, smiling. "And I cleaning your room!" he added, still smiling. I put my foot on the floor, and it landed right in a pile of pink goo. And that's when I knew it was toothpaste. Wolfie was wiping my floor with toothpaste and Kleenex. And there was toothpaste all over my bookshelf and my dresser. There was even some toothpaste on my lava lamp. I tried to pick up a Kleenex, but it was stuck to my floor.

And that's when I started to cry. Because Panda was empty and my gum was gone and I didn't get one single ridged chip dipped in Magic Midnight Fondue last night and now my room looked like it had been attacked by a mad dentist. Plus I had toothpaste coming out between my toes. I had to get out of there, so I wiped off my foot and put on some clothes and left Wolfie right where he was. I got on the bus without even eating breakfast.

"Your eyes are red," said Sharon.

"I know," I said. "My siblings are ruining my life." And then the crysies came again. Sharon handed me a Kleenex, and when I looked at it, I thought about Wolfie and the crysies came on harder. Bonnie looked at Sharon, and Sharon looked back at Bonnie. Then they both put their arms around me.

"I know how you feel," said Sharon.

"Really?" I said.

"Brothers are the worst." And as soon as Sharon said that, I thought about her

brothers—Hugo, Maynie, and Derek. I knew
that Sharon had to share her room with
Maynie every time her grandmother came.
She must have been through some hard times.

"Sisters are bad too," said Bonnie. "Especially half sisters." And as I thought about
Bonnie's half sister Becky, who had the loud-
est voice in the whole world, I knew she was
telling the truth.

Evan turned around and handed me a
strawberry fruit leather.

I said, "thanks" and started sucking it. Even
though Evan didn't have siblings, it seemed
like he understood. And as I sat there between
Sharon and Bonnie and thought about Evan's
kind face (which I couldn't see from behind),

I began to get up my courage and determination. I was stronger than bubble-gum toothpaste and Kleenex. I, Donahue Penelope Schneider, was going to find a way to make the annoying siblings stop ruining our lives. I was going to find a way to win this battle for all of us . . . including me.

CHAPTER TWELVE

FREEDOM DOES NOT COME FOR FREE

After lunch, I decided that Mrs. Howdy Doody and I were psychically connected, because when we were all seated she said, "Sometimes it's necessary to survive very difficult times to win your freedom." It was like she was speaking directly to me. "Some battles are won with weapons," Mrs. Howdy Doody said, "and some are won by willpower. Winning a difficult battle means enduring many hardships." Had she planned this lesson just for me? I had definitely lived through some very hard times lately.

Mrs. Howdy Doody moved her chair so that she was sitting directly in front of us. She took off her shoes and socks. "I have taken off my shoes and socks," she said. "Now it's time for you to take off yours." We all took off our socks and shoes, except for Emily, who had on tights. "Now close your eyes," she said. I was glad she told us to close our eyes, because her feet were very big, very white, and very ugly. She began speaking in a low, heavy voice.

> *"It is the winter of 1777.*
> *We are soldiers in the Continental Army,*
> *At Valley Forge.*
> *It's muddy, it's freezing,*
> *So freezing the mud is almost frozen,*
> *And it's so cold it hurts to take a breath.*
> *Everyone around you is sick.*
> *Everyone around you is hungry.*
> *Everyone around you is dirty."*

But then she switched to her regular voice and said, "Now, arise, ye sick, hungry, dirty soldiers! It's time to march." I didn't really feel like getting up after that poem stuff, but I knew a "no-choice" thing when I heard one.

"Here are your orders! Billy, Charlotte R., Tammy S., Sharon S., and Evan C. You will cross your arms and shiver as you march," said Mrs. Howdy Doody. Billy started making a *brrrr* noise right away. (He sounded kind of like a helicopter.) "Donnie," she said, "you will play the drum." Mrs. Howdy Doody handed Donnie a drum. Donnie looked happy.

"Amy D., Dessert, Jeanne S., Pat D., and Marshall W.," she said. "You will sneeze and cough as you march." It seemed like I always ended up in the same group as Amy D. "Jack S., Geezy Lou, Sam C., and Bonnie A., you are hungry, so you will growl." Jack was tiny, but he growled so loudly he sounded like a tiger.

"Grace E., Lois Z., Melissa R., and Michael A., you are filthy," Mrs. Howdy Doody continued. "Lois and Melissa, scratch your heads." Melissa started scratching so hard I thought her head really did itch. "Michael and Grace, you will plug your noses. Josh M., you suffer from all the afflictions," she said. "You will moan." Josh didn't seem too pleased about moaning. (I would have traded places with him in a second.)

"Now march, ye soldiers of Valley Forge, march despite the wind." Just then Mrs. Howdy Doody started blowing across the top of a bottle, and it really did sound like the wind. I had no idea she could do that.

And then I heard a very loud coughing right in my ear. I recognized Amy D.'s voice even though it was only a cough, so I turned around and fake-sneezed right in her face. She coughed even louder, but then Mrs. Howdy Doody started singing "My Country, 'Tis of Thee" and we all grew quiet.

When she finished singing, she said, "That beautiful song may not have been written until more than a half century after Valley Forge, but those words cry out to be heard! LET FREEDOM RING!" Mrs. Howdy Doody picked up her big bell and rang it. Then she said, "Attention, troops. You may return to your positions." Evan knew what she meant and walked straight to his desk, so the rest of us went to our desks too. And once we were sitting down again, Mrs. Howdy Doody said, "Freedom does not come for free, my dear happy learners. Freedom does not come for free."

CHAPTER THIRTEEN

KLEENEX STICKERS

I couldn't get "My Country, 'Tis of Thee" out of my head, and I hummed it all the way out of the classroom, down the hall, and onto the bus. I kept humming when I sat down. Sometimes it's really hard to get a song out of your head. Bonnie and Sharon asked me to be quiet. So I stopped humming and said to them, "You may leave your shoes on, but close your eyes for a moment." Once I saw that their eyes were closed, I said very softly,

"We are in our houses,
With our brothers,
And our sisters,
Our half sisters, too.
Charlie and Wolfie and Mushy,
Hugo and Maynie and Derek,
And the loud one, Becky.
My friends,
Listen to my words:
LET FREEDOM RING!"

Then I started humming "My Country, 'Tis of Thee" again.

"Dessert," said Sharon. "That's not funny."

"I'm not joking," I replied. "I'm going to free us from our annoying siblings."

89

"How are you going to do it?" said Sharon. "It's six against one when my brothers each have a friend over."

Bonnie opened her eyes and said, "Nothing will get Becky to stop making fun of me."

"Becky does not scare me," I said.

"I think I'm safe," said Evan, "because it's only me."

"Nobody's safe," I replied. "I used to be an only child too." Evan knew what I meant, and his face turned gray.

I didn't mean to worry him, but it was true. I was an only child for four years before Charlie showed up. "There must be a way to make our lives better," I said. "And I'm going to find it." There just had to be a way.

Pam was babysitting when I got home. "Did you see my room?" I said to her.

"I *heard* about your room," she replied.

"I bet Wolfie didn't even get yelled at," I said. I was sure I was right, because my parents never yell at the Beasties. I'm not sure how old you have to be to start getting in trouble, but I hope it happens to Wolfie soon.

"I just heard those Kleenex stickers were hard to get off," said Pam.

"Stickers?" I asked. "They weren't stickers."

"Well, they sure did stick to your floor with

all that toothpaste," said Pam, making cross-eyes at me.

And then I got a tingling feeling all over. I felt like a fairy had touched my brain. Stickers were exactly what I needed. Sometimes a little help comes when you least expect it.

"How do you start a club?" I asked Pam.

"A club?" she said. "I never started one. But I guess you just find people with a common interest, collect dues to cover expenses, and have meetings!"

"And you give them stickers," I said.

"Sure." Pam nodded. I know that sometimes people say "sure" just to make you happy, but I didn't care. I didn't care at all. I had everything I needed to make a club. My friends and I had annoying siblings, and I wanted to make them be nice.

As I headed upstairs, I thought about the club. I knew that Sharon and Bonnie would want to join, and maybe my lunch friends, too. I could be the president and they could pay me dues. Freedom from annoying siblings was not going to come for free. I knew I could solve this problem. I just didn't know how . . . yet.

Most clubs had some kind of special sign—some even had uniforms, like the Girl Scouts. I wasn't good at drawing people, but

I was good at letters. So I got out some paper and drew *A* for Annoying, *S* for Siblings, and *C* for Club.

The

A

S

C

Once I had drawn all the letters, I saw that it looked kind of like an annoying sibling. Mummy would have said it was meant to be.

I had some of Mummy's gold seals from a box of note cards she never used, so I drew the logo on each one with a black Sharpie. That way I knew it wouldn't rub off. They were the perfect stickers for my club. They almost looked like they came from a store. I put them in my backpack for Monday and practically whistled my way down the stairs. My future looked a lot brighter than it had this morning.

CHAPTER FOURTEEN

THE ANNOYING SIBLINGS CLUB

"Hugo called Muffy a boy," said Sharon when I got on the bus on Monday. "Then he drew a mustache on her." Muffy was Sharon's favorite doll because she could talk, and the mustache right on her mouth must have made Sharon feel really sad. But I patted Sharon on the knee and said, "Don't worry. Wolfie squeezed honey all over my hairbrush. Things always get worse before they get better." I patted her on the knee again and said, "I have good news to announce at lunch."

A few hours later I sat down at my lunch table, and before I even opened my lunch box,

I laid out the gold stickers. "What are those?" said Emily.

"The gold stickers are for people who join the Annoying Siblings Club," I said. "I'm the president."

Emily looked puzzled, so I said to her, "Are your sisters mean?"

97

"Maureen is nice," she said. "But Devon spies on me and Randi always gets her way."

"That's because Randi's the baby," I said. Then I told her that Devon sounded very annoying and that she'd better watch out for Maureen. "Annoying sibling can act like a disease," I said. "It can spread."

Emily looked concerned, so I continued, "I'm going to solve your annoying sibling problems, if you join my club."

"I'll join," said Emily. I did a little *phew* inside, because I knew it would be smooth sailing after that.

"Sharon?"

"Too late for me," said Sharon. "You know my brothers have it already."

"But I'm going to cure it," I said.

"Then I guess I'll join," said Sharon. Hugo and Maynie and Derek would be challenging, but they couldn't be worse than my own siblings.

I asked Evan, and he said, "I don't want to end up like Sharon. I'm in."

"Bonnie?"

"Can you get Becky to stop calling me names?"

"Piece o' cake," I said. (I couldn't believe I already had three members!)

I turned to Billy and Donnie, and before I even asked, Billy said, "Donnie's annoying when he pretends he's me."

"Same here," said Donnie. "I want to join."

And then Billy said he did too, so I said, "Great!" Then I looked at my friends and said, "There's just one more thing. Before I can give you all your stickers, you'll have to pay your dues."

"Dues?" said Emily.

"Freedom from annoying siblings is not free," I said, and I explained to them that the dues were three dollars per member and one

dollar per annoying sibling. Then I looked at Bonnie and said, "It's only fifty cents for a half sister." Bonnie nodded.

"You mean six dollars just for me?" asked Emily.

"Yes," I said, though Emily's questions were starting to make me a little nervous. "The money will cover expenses."

"Seems like a lot," said Emily. "But okay. I'll bring it tomorrow." I knew she wouldn't be disappointed.

"Do we have to pay?" said Billy.

"Three dollars together," I said. "Because you're twins." Getting Billy and Donnie to stop pretending to be each other couldn't be that hard.

"I didn't know about the dues," said Sharon. "But I have the money at home."

"It's a week's allowance for me," said Bonnie. "But it's worth it." (She didn't know how lucky she was to even *get* an allowance.)

Evan always carries his wallet, and he handed me three dollars right then. (I guess he was really scared.)

"I'll give you a receipt," I said, and ripped off a piece of my napkin. I wrote:

Name: Evan C.
Amount: $3.00
Received by:
Dessert Schneider

And then I gave Evan a gold sticker and started doing some mental addition. The way I figured, tomorrow I would get six dollars from Emily, six dollars from Sharon, three dollars from Billy and Donnie, and three dollars and fifty cents from Bonnie. Plus I already had Evan's three. That totaled twenty-one dollars and fifty cents. I put my hand in my pocket and felt those dollar bills. Then my fingers crumpled them into a wonderful little ball. I couldn't wait to put one into Panda. Even though they wouldn't make him clink or clank, at least he would know I was thinking about him.

"I'll collect your dues at lunch tomorrow," I said. I was so glad everybody had joined. Now I was going to be president of a real club!

CHAPTER FIFTEEN

COLLECTING DUES

I wore my cargo pants the next day, even though they're not "school clothes." I needed the big pockets for the money. But when I got on the bus, Sharon said, "Hugo cut Muffy's hair." And then her face turned bright pink and her eyes looked wet.

"Bring Muffy tomorrow," I said. "She can sleep at my house for now." I saw a few tears start to come down, and I wasn't sure if it was the right time to ask about dues, but I handed her a Kleenex and said, "Do you have your money?" She gave me a five and a one.

I looked her straight in the eyes and said, "We'll win this battle."

Bonnie handed me three dollars and fifty cents, most of it in change. "Don't worry about Becky," I said, putting the money in my side pocket.

It wasn't even eight o'clock in the morning and I already had nine dollars and fifty cents. This was going to be a piece o' cake. I got out my notebook and wrote out two receipts.

Name: Sharon S.
Amount: $6.00
Received by:
Dessert Schneider

I gave them each a gold sticker with the logo on it. Sharon put hers on her collar and Bonnie put hers on her arm. Evan's was already on his jacket.

I saw Billy and Donnie with Pat D. in the hall, and they each gave me a dollar fifty. I knelt down, got some more paper out of my backpack, and wrote out two more receipts.

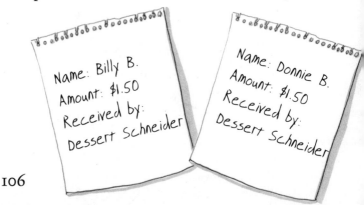

Then I gave them each a sticker.

"Can I get one too?" asked Pat.

"Do you have annoying siblings?" I said.

Pat told me he was an only child. Then he added, "But I have a dog, Peanut." I didn't know what could be wrong with having a dog, so I asked if Peanut was annoying.

"He's a thief," said Pat.

That made me think it was only fair to let Pat in the club, so I said, "Do you have four dollars?"

"I have snack money," he said, holding up two dollars. I figured Pat had the freedom to choose how to spend his money, so I said, "Half price cause it's just a dog. Two dollars is okay."

Pat handed me the bills, and I gave him

a sticker. I was writing out Pat's receipt when Melissa R. came by and said, "What are those gold things?"

"I'm president of the Annoying Siblings Club," I said. "You get one of those when you join." Then I asked her if she had any brothers or sisters who were ruining her life.

"My brother Jordan," she said.

I was feeling very confident, so I said, "Well, I can fix your problem if you pay me four dollars."

"I have ten dollars for the book fair," said Melissa. She was so lucky to have book fair money. My parents always make me get my books from the library. "Do you want solutions?" I said. "Or do you want some books?"

Melissa decided she could still get something good for the six dollars she'd have left, and she handed her dues to me. I took a five, gave her back a one, wrote out her receipt, and put a sticker right on the front of her shirt. I was so happy Melissa and Pat had joined. That was six dollars more than I had planned. Emily was the only one left, and I'd get her dues at lunch. I had twenty-one fifty already! I glided through the morning because my future was starting to glow.

At lunch I asked Emily if she had brought her dues.

"I did," she said, and handed me her six dollars. "Do I get a refund if this doesn't work?"

"Listen," I answered, as I put her gold sticker on her shirt. "There's a lot of work to do here. We're going to take it one step at a time." Then I told everybody we'd hold our first meeting at lunch tomorrow. I couldn't wait to get started.

Name: Pat D.
Amount: $2.00
Received by:
Dessert Schn

Name: Melissa R.
Amount: $4.00
Received by:
...neider

Name: Emily V.
Amount: $6.00
Received by:
Dessert Schneider

CHAPTER SIXTEEN

THE BOOK FAIR

That afternoon our class had its turn at the book fair. And I realized that if I was going to run a meeting, I needed a new notebook, and it could be an "expense," just like Pam had said. The book fair was in the library, so when we walked in the door, I took a left because it looked like that was where they were selling "extra" stuff. I looked carefully, but I didn't see any regular notebooks. Lucky for me, they did have "journals." And they were really pretty. I was trying to decide between the one with kittens and the one with smiley faces, but then I saw one with cupcakes on the front, five big colored cupcakes with sprinkles on top! Even though it was fifty cents more than the others, it felt a little thicker, so I decided it was worth it. I would probably need the extra room to write down everybody's problems. I headed up to the checkout, and right there in front of me were some beautiful pens with flags on the ends. And that made me think about being president. It seemed only right that I have a presidential pen to take my notes tomorrow. And they were only a dollar. So I picked up a flag pen. But then I saw a pen that could write in eight different colors. I had seen pens that could write in six colors before, but never one with *eight*.

And I had exactly eight members in my club. Sometimes things happen for a reason. And I realized right then that the reason the pen was sitting there was because it wanted me to buy it. It was two fifty, so my total came to seven dollars and fifty cents. And I still had tons of money left. Not only that, but now I, President Donahue Penelope Schneider, was fully prepared for the meeting. Everything was going so smoothly, and I was going to make my friends' lives better . . . mine already was!

CHAPTER SEVENTEEN

MY LITTLE HEAP OF MONEY

After school, as soon as I got to my room, I took off my cargo pants and turned them upside down. I shook them to get the money out. The coins came out first, and they rolled around and around. I didn't see any dollars, but I knew I had some, so I put my hand in the pockets and loosened up a few. I shook again. I watched as two five-dollar bills and quite a few ones made their way out of my pockets and landed safely on the floor.

And that little pile of money made me

very happy. I gathered all the change and put it into Panda, but I kept the bills out, just in case there was another trip to the bank or something even worse. Panda began to clink and clank like he did in the old days. It was good to see his dark eyes with a tiny bit of gleam in them again.

When Mummy called me to set the table, I hollered, "Be right down." But I didn't move. She always yells again pretty quickly, like the snooze button on my alarm clock. I don't usually go till the third time. But a few minutes later, Charlie walked in.

"Get out," I said.

"We're having Lime Meltaways," Charlie said. "Mummy let me be the critic." Her face looked like a squinchy little rodent's, and she added, "Because I set the table for you."

I walked right over to her until I was one inch away. My head was a whole head above hers, and I put my hands on her shoulders and squeezed just a little and said, "GET OUT OF MY ROOM."

Charlie backed out, but when she got to the stairs she looked back at me and hissed. Then she said, "I'm telling."

I didn't even care if the rodent told on me, because there was nothing to tell anyway, plus I was president and I had a little heap of money. Panda was happy again too. So what if Charlie got to taste the Lime Meltaways first. . . . There were eight members in my club, and I was going to make their lives better.

At supper, Daddy said, "Dom wants to know if you're coming to Fondue this weekend." Dom does most of the restaurant baking on Saturdays, and sometimes I help.

"Tell her I can't wait," I said. That was the truth. I needed to get away from those three—the rodent, the toothpaste gluer, and the fondue spiller.

And then we ate our Lime Meltaways, and after that we had chicken pot pie, and the carrots and peas and chicken inside their snug pie house were like thick creamy soup. I couldn't wait to help Dom. I wasn't sure what sweet treats we'd be making together, but I knew I'd be the critic.

CHAPTER EIGHTEEN

THE FIRST MEETING

On the bus the next morning Sharon was sitting next to Muffy. My heart twisted a little bit when I looked at the doll.

She had very little hair, and her face was covered with Magic Marker. She had a hole in her back where her talk box had been. But I tried not to make a face as I put her legs up over her head so she fit in my backpack, and I said, "Don't worry, Sharon. I'll take care of her." From the looks of things, Hugo was even worse than Wolfie. I had my work cut out for me.

On the way to our classroom, Amy D. stopped me. "I have an annoying sibling," she said. "Let me in your club."

"No way," I replied. "You *are* an annoying sibling." (If ever there was an annoying sibling, it was Amy D.)

"Give me a sticker," she said.

There was zero chance Amy D. was getting a sticker. "No sticker," I said, "and that's final."

"You'll be sorry," she said.

But I knew in my heart that I would never be sorry for not letting Amy D. in my club, so I moved a step back and said, "Never."

When I got to our room, Mrs. Howdy Doody was not wearing her colonial outfit. (I had gotten kind of used to it.) So I said, "Good morning, Mrs. Howdy Doody."

"Good morning, Dessert," she said. It was a little weird to be called plain old Dessert and not

Colonist Schneider, but we were moving on to Earth studies. I was moving on too, and pretty soon I would be holding my first meeting! It seemed to take forever to get to 11:50, but finally we were on our way to the cafeteria, and Pat and Melissa squeezed in at our table.

"Our meeting is called to order," I said. "It's time to share our problems." I ate a few bites from my garbage can while I set out my notebook and my eight-color pen. I needed both hands, so I didn't even bother plugging my nose. The first thing I did was take attendance. "President Schneider," I called

123

out. Then I said, "Here." Everybody laughed, which I figured meant we were off to a great start. I went through the rest of the members, and our attendance was 100 percent. "I'll pick the first person," I said. "And after that person shares, they can pick the next one. Emily, you go first!" I decided to use orange for Emily.

"I was just trying on some of my mom's necklaces," said Emily, "and Devon told on me, and I got a 'warning.' Randi does it all the time and never gets in trouble."

As I was writing down Emily's problem, I was thinking about a solution. I knew that the "babies" never get in trouble, so I focused on Devon. I knew exactly what to say. This was going to be a piece o' cake.

"Stop, look, listen, and hide," I said. And I explained to her that she has to STOP before she goes into her mom's room, LOOK to make sure no one's watching, LISTEN for any noises, and if anybody was coming, HIDE.

"As for Randi," I said, "that's harder. The babies never get blamed." I told her I'd have to think about that. Emily looked satisfied, so I wrote, "*stop, look, listen, and hide*" next to her problem. Then Emily chose Donnie.

Donnie pointed at Billy and said, "Mom told him to clear the table and he pretended he was me." Then Billy pointed at Donnie and said, "Same. Then we *both* had to clear."

This was an interesting problem. I clicked

through each color on my pen, and by the time I finished, I had the solution!

"Just write your names on your shirts with a Sharpie!" I said. Billy and Donnie thought that sounded good.

"Two down, six to go." I picked red for Donnie and blue for Billy and wrote, "label shirts" next to each of their problems. I knew that Billy and Donnie's situation wasn't as serious as some of the others, but it was still a good sign that I had a solution already.

"I choose Melissa," said Billy.

"Jordan takes my money," said Melissa. "And my parents don't believe it."

"Hmm," I said, choosing green for Melissa. "When you get home, write your initials on your money. At least if he takes it, you'll have evidence." I wrote down, "Initial money."

"That's a good idea," said Melissa. "I choose Sharon."

"You have Muffy," said Sharon, and I swallowed hard as I thought of Muffy in my backpack.

With the purple pen, I started to write down Sharon's problem, "Hugo, Maynie, Derek, Muffy, markers, scissors," but then I stopped and said to her, "Your problem is larger. But you can start by taking away the Magic Markers and the scissors so your brothers can't attack another doll."

"Okay," said Sharon. "I pick Bonnie."

I was very surprised when Bonnie started speaking loudly. "Becky says I have lice, and she takes my tooth-fairy prizes before I wake up, and she's babysitting me tonight, and when she wants my food she sneezes on my plate to contaminate it so I won't eat it. She hogs the phone, and then she lied—"

"Brush it off, Bonnie. Brush it off," I said. I had picked pink for Bonnie, and I was trying to keep up with her but she talked too fast. "Becky's only one person," I said. "And we are going to fix it." I had just heard more words out of Bonnie's mouth than I had heard from her in my entire life. I didn't know she could talk that much. But she calmed down when I interrupted, and she said, "All right. I pick Evan." I wrote down "brush it off,"and then I said, "There's no need for Evan to share today." I was feeling presidential. I continued, "He doesn't have siblings at this time." I jotted down, "no siblings yet" in yellow. Then I asked Evan who he picked, even though there was only one person left.

Evan said, "Pat."

Pat told us that Peanut had stolen the bacon right off his BLT. I gave this some thought, and I realized that if Peanut liked bacon, it would be hard to keep him away from it.

"A lettuce-tomato sandwich is very different from a bacon-lettuce-tomato sandwich," I said. "Let Peanut outside before supper." Then

- Stop, look, listen, and hide

Donnie

Billy

label shirts

- Initial money (M)

- Hugo, Maynie, Derek, Muffy, markers, scissors

- brush it off

no siblings yet

peanut out

toolbox
kleenex
magic midnight

I wrote down "*peanut out*" in light blue. I knew it wasn't the most exciting plan in the world, but I didn't see how it could fail, and Pat seemed to agree.

I took my regular black pen out of my pocket (because all the other colors were gone) and wrote "*toolbox, Kleenex, magic midnight*" at the bottom of the page so I wouldn't forget about myself. And then I said, "Thank you for a wonderful meeting! Billy and Donnie will label their clothes, Emily will follow my instructions, Pat will let Peanut out, Melissa will initial her money, and Sharon will take away the weapons. Bonnie, brush it off. I'll get back to you tomorrow morning."

I felt tired from all that talking and

listening, and a little thirsty. I went over to the school store. It was always right there in the cafeteria, but I'd never thought about making a purchase before. I bought myself a Lambert Elementary School water bottle and filled it with water at the fountain. It was only two dollars, and I had earned it. I was well on my way to solving all the problems—I just had to figure out the ones that were still a puzzle. I had some thinking to do.

CHAPTER NINETEEN

THE MENU

Mummy was nowhere to be seen when I walked in from school, so I went straight upstairs, unzipped my backpack, held it upside down, and shook. Muffy came out, still all curled up. I picked her up and straightened out her legs, but I could barely look her in the eyes. "You'll be safe in my drawer," I said. But the hole in her back felt like a wound, so I held her facing out with the hole pressed against my shirt. I dumped all the papers and stuff out of my drawer and laid her in there. "Panda's here," I whispered to her. "He'll keep watch over you." But as she lay there, she seemed like she might be in a coma. And not the kind of coma you wake up from. I was a little worried.

I started to gather up all the stuff I'd dumped out, and I couldn't believe what I found—Bernie, a little baby Chihuahua I'd thought was lost forever. I carefully picked him up. I loved him even more than I remembered. Sometimes that's how it is when you lose something I guess. I put him in the tiny crate with my other china dogs. Charlie had probably been playing with him when I wasn't home and stuck him in my drawer when she heard Mummy coming. Next I tried to straighten out the big pile of papers without getting a paper cut, when my eyes caught sight of something blue with little squares all over it. It was the hot-lunch menu. I must have put it in there so I wouldn't be reminded of my stinkin' Thermos. Thinking about that Thermos made me want hot lunch more than ever. And now that I thought about it, I realized it could just be another expense. I was so grateful to have some money again. So I lay down on my bed with Chunky and took a peek at the menu. I covered up all the days except tomorrow. Then I read, *French Toast Soldiers with Maple Syrup, 100 percent beef sausage* (not mystery meat), *Jell-O with whipped cream* (I knew this came with a Maraschino cherry), *and fresh fruit* (I was pretty sure you could get an apple). I felt like it was designed just for me, breakfast food for lunch. It was almost too good to be true.

I figured I would go ahead and check out

the rest of the menu too, because I could definitely afford it. Friday was Festival of Nachos or Jambilicious PB&J. Both of those sounded delicious. They sounded so much better than mystery meat. I noticed that I could substitute Jambilicious PB&J every single day if I wanted to. Now I knew what Mrs. Howdy Doody meant about the freedom to choose. I hugged the hot-lunch menu tight.

Then I did my homework and tried to think about what Bonnie should do. It sounded bad. I knew I'd told her to "brush it off," but that was really just to get her to stop talking. It seemed to me that her best chance was to get Becky out of the house entirely— maybe to her friend's house, or on a trip, or maybe even to the hospital. I thought this was the right approach, I just had to figure out exactly how we could do it.

And the next thing I knew was that the smell of pizza filled my room—Mummy's homemade pizza. And Wolfie appeared and said, "Pizza!" This was going to be the perfect ending to a perfect day, except for Muffy. But at least she was safely tucked away in my drawer. I couldn't wait for that pizza, because even though I'd be eating French Toast Soldiers tomorrow, I was hungry today.

CHAPTER TWENTY

HOT LUNCH

Sharon looked terrible the next morning. "You forgot to say take away the glue," she said. "They glued my dollhouse door shut."

"This is a challenge," I said. "Let me see." I knew that glue was hard to get off, so I had to come up with a different idea.

"At least Muffy is safe." I said. "Do you think your parents would let you have a lock on the door to your room?"

"Probably not," said Sharon.

"Just ask," I said, but I wasn't very hopeful.

Parents always like to know what we're doing.

And then I turned to Bonnie and said, "We've got to get Becky out of the house. I'm just about ready to share my plan." Even though she was talking like crazy lately, Bonnie was the most patient of all my friends, and she said she'd wait for my plan.

The morning went by pretty quickly, and at 11:50 when we lined up for lunch and Mrs. Howdy Doody opened the door, I didn't just smell hot lunch in the air . . . I smelled *my* hot lunch in the air. To be standing here, about to taste the French Toast Soldiers for the first time in my life, was worth all of the sacrifices I'd made along the way. I felt like I could solve any problem in the world if it meant I could stand here smelling that wonderful syrupy, buttery, delicious food that I was about to get to eat.

I went through the line with Donnie and Billy (they always buy vanilla milk). It was especially nice to be with them, because I thought the French Toast Soldiers looked kind of like twins too, just the two of them lying in that white cardboard basket. And the 100 percent beef sausages looked so happy together. I got green Jell-O, and the Maraschino cherry was right there in the very center of the whipped cream as if it were specially designed for me. The apple was kind of small, but all the bananas had brown spots on them so I took it. Most important, I had the freedom to choose. So I chose chocolate milk over orange juice and took an invisible curtsy because I, Dessert Schneider, was about to eat hot lunch!

I sat down at our table and placed the tray in front of me.

The first thing I ate was my Maraschino cherry. Even though I've had quite a few Mara-

schino cherries in my life, there was something about this one that was more delicious. I think it was more delicious because it was on top of the green Jell-O, and the green Jell-O was the dessert part of the hot lunch, and I've been dreaming about hot lunch for years. I ate the Jell-O itself next, and it slid right down my throat. And then came the twin soldiers. I dunked the first one in my maple syrup, took a bite, and chewed as slowly as I could because I wanted it to last forever. Then I dunked it again (it didn't matter that I was double-dipping, because I had it all to myself). Soldier Number Two was next, and I double-dipped him exactly the same way. When he was gone I still had a little bit of syrup left, so I dipped my beef sausages in as if they were soldiers. They tasted good. I ate the apple and drank my chocolate milk. When I finally looked up, Emily said, "I hope your hot lunch wasn't an 'expense.'"

I wasn't going to tell her it *was* an expense after she said that, so I just asked her if she had stopped, looked, listened, and hid.

"Maureen's a problem now too, Dessert," she said.

This was a very bad sign for me. Maureen was Emily's only nice sister. "She has to make my breakfast," Emily continued, "and she put orange juice in my cereal instead of milk." This was not supposed to happen. I wasn't quite sure what to say, but I didn't want Emily to know that. I had to come up with something, but what? And then I got it.

"Eat your cereal dry for now."

Pat didn't even wait for Emily to say

anything back. "Peanut wouldn't go out," he said. "It was raining."

Hmm. I hadn't considered the weather. Of course Peanut didn't want to get wet. But lucky for me it wasn't raining today, so I said, "Well, it's sunny now. Try the plan tonight." (I prayed that it would work.)

Then I looked at Melissa and said, "Did you initial your money?"

"All of it," she said.

"Then it's just a waiting game now," I said. I was sure Jordan would get caught.

"We labeled all our shirts," said Billy, "with a Sharpie."

"Good," I said. "Your names will not come out."

I turned to Evan and said, "No news is good news." He smiled at me.

I was making progress, but I still had a long road ahead of me. It definitely wasn't going to be a piece o' cake like I thought, but I was confident I could find some solutions that would work. Muffy was safe for now, but Sharon's problem was huge, and I didn't really think her parents would let her get a lock. Then I had to get Becky out of Bonnie's house. But I was almost certain Peanut would go outside tonight, so Pat was taken care of, and Donnie and Billy were all set too. Melissa's brother would probably walk right into the "initial trap," so she'd have evidence shortly, and Evan was still alone, which was how he wanted it. But I was worried about Emily. I hadn't expected Maureen to turn on her, and I didn't like what she'd said about my expenses. If only I could "train" all these siblings the way I've trained Chunky. But one thing I know is that people don't learn as fast as Chunky does.

CHAPTER TWENTY-ONE

A FESTIVAL OF NACHOS?

The first thing I did when I got up the next morning was to take a look at the hot-lunch menu again—it was still a tie between the Festival of Nachos and the Jambilicious PB&J. But I remembered that I could always substitute the PB&J, so I decided to go with the nachos. Then I got dressed and gave Panda a jingle. He sounded perky, so I poked my head in Muffy's drawer. But when I opened it, I thought she looked worse than ever. Maybe she didn't like being in the dark. I sat her up on my bookshelf so she could look around. She seemed a little better up there.

When I went down to get my breakfast, Dad asked me why I hadn't eaten my lunch the day before. So I told him I hadn't been hungry, which was like telling the truth and lying at the same time. I didn't feel that great about it, but I didn't really want to mention the French Toast Twins from yesterday or the Festival of Nachos I was planning to try today. So I left it at that.

Sharon was shaking her head no when I got on the bus. "No lock?" I said.

"No lock," she answered. "And I miss Muffy."

"I could bring Muffy back," I told her. "Do you want her back?"

Sharon nodded.

"Okay," I said.

Bonnie didn't look good either. She shook her hair and some white and black stuff came out. And then she told the story of how Becky said she was going to give her real "lice" and had shaken salt and pepper in her hair just before she got on the bus. It sounded disgusting. When I started the club, I knew my friends' siblings were annoying, but I didn't know their problems were this bad. I could hardly stand to think about it. My friends' problems seemed to be getting worse instead of better. This wasn't as easy as I thought it would be, and there was this little tiny part of me that was beginning to think I might not win.

But my spirits picked up when I remembered the Festival of Nachos I was going to be eating. And soon enough, lunchtime came. I went through the line with Billy and Donnie again, and at first the nachos looked exciting. But when I got closer, I wasn't really sure why they called it a "festival." There was a pile of chips with a little tub of orange cheese and some black olives and lettuce and tomatoes. The lettuce looked old (it was "rusty" around the edges). So I took a side of mozzarella sticks just in case—it was only one dollar more. I also got a big chocolate chip cookie and some strawberry milk.

We sat down, and I had just barely put a bite of cookie in my mouth before Emily said, "Dry cereal tastes like cat food, Dessert."

Then Pat said, "Peanut went outside, but she went straight into the garage and chewed up my Frisbee. She took it right off its hook."

If I had known Peanut would be so annoying, I never would have given Pat the discount. The problems were getting worse. I pointed to my full mouth to buy myself some time, but Emily said, "I want my money back. Even Randi could have thought of your dry-cereal solution." I wanted to tell Emily that taking the liquid away was just a temporary measure until I thought of the real solution, but I didn't think she was in the mood to listen. She hadn't

153

given me much of a chance at all. It didn't seem fair that she wanted her money back already.

Then Melissa said, "Guess what, Dessert? Jordan wrote his initials all over my money too. Now I'll never be able to prove anything." I didn't know Melissa's brother was that smart, so I said, "I didn't expect that. Let me think." But inside I was worried. I thought my plan for Jordan would work. I wasn't sure I could think of another. I took a tortilla chip and dipped it in the cheese. But a little bit of the "old" lettuce got in with the cheese, so I set the chip down and picked out the lettuce. This lunch was going badly.

"Ours didn't work either," said Billy. "Donnie wore my 'Billy' shirt."

"And he wore mine," said Donnie. And then they explained how they both had to clear the table again and that they also got grounded for using permanent marker. I put another chip in my mouth. It wasn't even crispy. This was definitely not a "festival," the way the menu said. But at least I still had the side of mozzarella sticks.

And that's when Amy D. came over to our table. She took a mozzarella stick, dipped it in my sauce, and bit off the

end. Then she picked up the whole container of sticks, and when I reached to grab them back, something very warm landed in my lap.

"Oops," she said. "Sorry about your marinara sauce."

Amy walked away, and my friends just kept talking. Nobody even seemed to care about what happened to me. I didn't feel at all like a president. My dress had a big red stain all over the front of it, and I had seven problems I couldn't solve. I wouldn't be surprised if Evan's parents told him they were going to have triplets next.

"Does anybody have a napkin?" I said. And nothing appeared, except for Bonnie's brown paper lunch bag. I tried to use it to get the red sauce off my dress, but it just spread some more. Then I went to the sink to wash it off. That didn't work either, and now my dress was all wet. I looked bad, I felt worse, and I still had to sit through the long afternoon. I didn't ever want to see another nacho or mozzarella stick again in my whole life.

CHAPTER TWENTY-TWO

FROM BAD TO WORSE

I knew that I had told Sharon things always get worse before they get better, but as I walked into my house from the bus, with that big stain on the front of my dress, I didn't really think things could get much worse. Then the phone started ringing. I picked it up and said, "Schneider residence."

"Hello, Theresa? It's Maggie Rheingold. I'm calling about your daughter." (Theresa is Mummy's name. Mrs. Rheingold must have thought I was Mummy.)

"Yes?" (I figured I might as well find out what she wanted.)

"She's taking people's money at school. She took my daughter Melissa's book-fair money. Something about a sticker." This could not be good for me.

"I'm sorry," I said. "I'll look into that." (Even though I tried to sound chirpy, the insides of me felt like a milkshake.)

Mrs. Rheingold said, "Thank you," and I got off the phone as fast as I could. Pam came downstairs and asked me who had called. I didn't want to say anything to Pam, because she might tell my parents, so I lied and said, "Wrong number." Then I went upstairs to try to start my homework, but I felt like there were rocks in my stomach.

Now I was worried. Melissa's mother did not sound nice, and I hadn't solved any problems. This wasn't working out like I hoped. I was trying my best for Sharon and Emily and Donnie and Billy and Pat and Bonnie and Melissa, but I was not getting results. Was there any way to fix things? I had to think, and I had to think hard. And that's when I noticed the empty space on my bookshelf. That's when I noticed that Muffy was gone. And that's when I noticed the upside-down wastebasket on the floor of my room, right in front of the bookcase.

"WOOOOOOOOOOL-FIEEEEEEEEEE!" I yelled. "WOOOOOOOOOOL-FIEEEEEEEE!" I had told Sharon I would give Muffy back. But I had no idea where she was. I had to find Muffy.

I didn't have to look very hard, because she showed up a few minutes later. In Wolfie's hands. Mushy was at his side, and they all smelled like nail polish. Wolfie's hands were green and sticky... and they stank. Muffy's hair,

or what was left of it, was full of bright green nail polish, and it was sticky-looking too. And there was nail polish all over her body.

The rodent came rushing in right behind them, yelling, "THAT'S MY NAIL POLISH!" But then she stopped when she saw Muffy. "You ruined Sharon's doll," she said. And when I looked closely at that doll, even though my brain knew that she didn't really have a heart in her chest or tears in her eyes, she felt real to me.

And she was near the end of her life.

I took her in my arms and I said, "I'm sorry." And a couple of tears came out, and they mixed with the nail polish, and Muffy got gooier and stickier than she was already. I looked at my siblings, one by one, and I knew then that I had no hope. If I couldn't even keep Sharon's doll safe in my own house, how could I ever fix everybody else's problems? What was I going to do? I couldn't even refund the dues, because I only had twelve dollars left.

CHAPTER TWENTY-THREE

TIPS

When I woke up Saturday morning, I didn't feel like getting out of bed. I was afraid to look at Muffy, but I felt like I had to. Her eyes were still closed. *Sharon's doll was dead.* I felt like I was dying too, but I knew that Dom was expecting my help this morning.

Somehow I managed to get dressed and I managed to eat some toast. And when Pam arrived, I managed to say a tiny, "Hello." And somehow I managed to get in the car with my parents. They must have been tired from working the night before because neither one of them was talking. I was grateful for the silence.

When we got to Fondue, Mummy went to the reservation book and Dad went back in the kitchen. I went straight to the pastry station. Dom handed me a rolling pin and a big ball of dough and said, "Cookie Braids." I guess we were making Cookie Braids today. Usually I'm excited about baking with Dom, but not today. All I could think of was paying back my friends, who didn't like me anymore. Where was I going to get the money? I kept my head down and my hands moving so Dom wouldn't ask me any questions.

Then Gaby came by, and she didn't look

like a new waiter anymore. She was smiling,
and she looked neat and clean. I guess she had
passed her training.

"Hi, Dessert," she said. "Long time no
see. Are you helping Dom today?"

I couldn't believe she was the same person I'd met last week. She
seemed so comfortable
now.

I looked up at
her, but no words
came out, so I looked
back down and kept
on rolling.

"What's the
matter?" Gaby

asked. I stopped rolling for a second and I looked at her.

"Everything," I said.

Dom was right behind us and said, "Can you roll and talk at the same time?"

"Sorry, Dom," I said, and I started rolling again, as fast as I could.

"We need a week's worth of Cookie Braids," she said. "It's graham crackers after that." She dropped another huge ball of yellow and brown dough on my table.

"Dom, I'm going as fast as—" and then my rolling pin slipped out from under my hands. I had never dropped a rolling pin before.

I think Dom knew things were bad, because she picked it up and said, "You need a break." Dom had never given me a break before.

I turned to Gaby and said, "I'm in trouble."

Gaby bent down and took my face in her hands. "Is there something I can do for you?"

"I don't think so," I said. "I need fifteen dollars and fifty cents."

And then Gaby took her hands off my face, and while I stood there watching her, she pulled a wad of money out of her apron pocket. It must have been her tips. She gave me a ten and a five and a one. "Pay me back when you can," she said.

"Are you going to tell my parents?" I asked. She shook her head and said, "Of course not.

Remember when you tied my apron for me?"

"Yes."

"That was just about the only reason I didn't quit that night."

"Really?" I said. And Gaby just nodded.

"What about me?" said Dom. "I made the bread that night."

"You did make the bread," said Gaby. "You're a good friend too." And I could tell from the way Gaby talked that she didn't mind that Dom had been listening the whole time.

Gaby hadn't even asked me what the money was for. She was so generous. I had only tied her apron that night because I felt sorry for her and I knew Guston was waiting. But Gaby hadn't forgotten.

My life had just done a U-turn. Gaby had loaned me the money. And my parents weren't going to find out. And even though I was going to have to tell my club I failed and give them back their dues, I thought I could do it. It wouldn't be the first time I'd had to apologize. There was just one thing that was still making my stomach jiggly. How was I going to tell Sharon, kindhearted Sharon who I sit with on the bus every day, what had happened to Muffy?

CHAPTER TWENTY-FOUR

THE WRONG CUSTOMER

But just as things were looking up for me, my life U-turned again, this time in the wrong direction. I heard Mummy's heels clacking. I looked up and there she was, and she did not look pleased. "Let me introduce you to a member of the Annoying Siblings Club," she said. "He's in the dining room."

And when she said that, my heart went straight down to my feet. Mummy put her hand around my fingers and pulled me away, even though my feet did not want to move.

In the dining room, at a small table by the fountain, sat Pat D., with his parents and what must also be his grandparents. His face made me think he didn't want to be there. His ASC sticker was on his shirt. Why, oh why, did Pat and his family have to come to Fondue today? Mummy's job is "front of house." That means she talks to everybody who walks in the door on the weekends. And that meant she probably knew everything by now.

"I was talking with Pat DeMarco," said Mummy, "and he told me he's in your club." Her face looked tight. "And he told me he paid you dues. What do you have to say about that?"

Then my dad came out of the kitchen,

with a spatula in his hand. I could tell from his eyes that Mummy had already talked to him. His eyes reminded me of how I'd lied to him about my Thermos, which reminded me that I had bought my hot lunch
with my friends' money,
the very same money
they had paid me

to solve their problems. Thinking about that hot lunch reminded me of how my friends didn't help clean up the marinara sauce Amy D. dumped on me, and now I understood why. Because I hadn't been a good friend to them.

And that felt the worst of all, and when I opened my mouth to say something it sounded like a frog was in there. "I wanted to fix our problems," I said to Mummy and Daddy. But then my knees turned into ice cream and I had to hold the back of Mrs. DeMarco's chair. "But I can't," I said quietly.

The tears were getting going now and I couldn't stop them. I started to wipe my face on my sleeve. And that's when Pat D. handed me a napkin, and that little act of kindness made it harder to talk. So I kept my mouth closed.

"On behalf of our entire family," said Mummy to the DeMarcos, "my apologies. Dessert will pay back the money and your meal is on the house." That's when I knew just how bad it was, because Mummy doesn't like giving food away for free.

She brought me home right after that, and she didn't say anything the whole way, until we were just about in our driveway. Then she said, "You can think about making things right while you clean out the van. And I don't want one spot left in there."

CHAPTER TWENTY-FIVE

CLEANING THE VAN

I was a little bit glad to have something to do, because I felt like I'd lost the war against annoying siblings and I'd lost my friends at the same time. I went in to get the cleaning stuff, and Chunky was waiting for me. He wagged his tail. "Let's get to work," I said to him. I put on my winter coat and I put on my gloves. I found the extension cord in the basement and I plugged in the vacuum. I went outside, and it was cold, but I knew what had to be done. I opened all the van doors and I went inside.

First I threw all the stuff I found in there into the driveway. There were lots of crayons and there were lots of old french fries. There were some mittens, and there were some baby wipes. There were old tissues and used straws.

There were some batteries and some candy wrappers. There was a lump of hardened sticky stuff that felt like frozen gum. I was afraid that one was mine. And there were paper clips, water bottles, and some green Goldfish. Those had to be Wolfie's, because he eats every color of Goldfish except green. I gathered everything into a big plastic bag and threw it out. Vacuuming was next. I heard metal going up the tube. But I kept right on vacuuming. A lot of stuff

was getting sucked up that hose.

I'd been vacuuming for some time, and I was getting tired, when I found a quarter under the floor mat. Staring right up at me was George Washington, and looking at him made me remember that I didn't have it half as bad as the Continental Army. I stuck the coin in my pocket and started on the windows.

But then, as the sun began to set, a small, dark figure appeared in the side window. I heard a knocking sound.

I opened the door and it was Charlie, one of my own annoying siblings, with April Showers in her arms. April is her favorite doll, and she kicks when you stick her in water. "I want to give April Showers to Sharon," she said. And she held the doll out toward me.

"Is this for your toolbox?" I asked Charlie.

"No," said Charlie. "It's for Sharon. Because Muffy's dead."

"Are you sure you want to give her away?"

And when Charlie nodded and said, "I don't play with her that much anymore," I knew she was telling the truth.

And I sat down in the backseat, and Charlie sat next to me, and for the first time in forever long, she wasn't being annoying, and she wasn't doing this for her toolbox.

"I have annoying siblings too," she said softly.

Charlie went back inside, and I finished the windows. Then I cleaned the rearview mirror too. That was extra. Next I went into the garage and found Daddy's car-cleaning bucket and sponges, and the special car soap. And I started scrubbing. I kept filling the bucket with hot water and it kept steaming from the cold. And as I scrubbed I kept thinking about what Charlie had said. I guess she did have annoying siblings. I kept thinking about what she'd done, too. She had given me April Showers for Sharon. She had done something nice that was going to make it a little easier to tell Sharon that Muffy's life was over. And then I climbed right up to the roof and polished that, too, because Mummy had said she wanted it spotless. That was really extra.

Mummy did come out to inspect a few minutes later, and she said, "That will do," which if I weren't in trouble would mean,

"Magnifique!" Then she said, "The bank will be next. You can withdraw enough money to pay everyone back."

And I just said, "Okay." For some reason, I didn't want to tell Mummy that Gaby had lent me her tip money. It was just between us, and I wanted to keep it that way. That seemed right.

CHAPTER TWENTY-SIX

THE END OF THE ASC

On Monday I waited until lunchtime to tell Sharon about Muffy, and when we all sat down at the table, I looked at her and said, "Muffy didn't make it."

Sharon put her lips together, and her eyes got big and her face got pink, like it always does when she's sad.

"But I have something for you," I said. "It's from my sister." And I handed her Charlie's doll. "Her name is April Showers."

Sharon's face was still pink. "She doesn't look like Muffy," she said.

"But she kicks when you put her in water," I replied.

"She does?" said Sharon, and I could see her lips start to stretch a little bit, like they were beginning to make a smile. She started smoothing down April's white hair so I said, "I hope your brothers leave her alone." I didn't know whether her brothers would cooperate or not, but I made a tiny wish that they would.

And then I looked at the rest of my friends and I knew that it was time to tell them that I couldn't solve their problems and they'd be getting a refund. But when I opened my mouth, all that came out was a creaky noise. I sounded like an engine that couldn't get going. Everybody was waiting. And I knew that if I didn't get the words out now, I never would and that I'd be stuck right where I was forever.

So I took the biggest breath I could and rubbed my Thermos between my hands and said, "The club is over. I'm giving you all a refund." Phew. My engine was going now, so I rubbed my Thermos harder and gathered all my courage, and I asked the question that scared me the most.

"Can I still be your friend?" I didn't know what the answer would be, but I was surprised how good it felt to have sent the question out to them.

And when I looked around the table, I saw that my friends were nodding. And I felt like the luckiest person in the world because I was pretty sure that they forgave me.

And then I gave Sharon her six dollars and Bonnie her three dollars and fifty cents. I gave Billy and Donnie each their dollar fifty. I gave Evan his three dollars, Melissa her four dollars, Pat his two dollars, and Emily her six dollars.

And once I had paid back my friends, I thought about Charlie. I couldn't wait to tell her that Sharon liked April Showers. I couldn't wait to tell her that April almost made Sharon smile, even though Muffy was dead, and that Sharon liked April's white hair. And I also wanted to tell her that if she ever missed April a lot, I would take her over to Sharon's for a visit.

Then I wanted to say one last thing, not

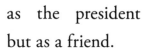

as the president but as a friend.

"I don't really know how to make siblings not annoying," I said. "But I do know that sometimes, just when you need them the most, they do something especially nice."

I guess Mummy was right after all. I guess you never do know exactly what's going to happen from one moment to the next.

ACKNOWLEDGMENTS

To those who believe in possibility, lots and lots of love

Christine, William, Kamille, Juliette, and Jacques Snell—my own first family of food

Emily van Beek, my agent, who said, "Stickers"

Kiley Frank, because she's an architect and an editor

McGhee Louise and Marshall Washington, thank you for the big belly laughs

Mrs. Normana Schaaf, who shines bright as a new penny

Jennifer Mills Brown, who used to sneeze on her brother's cereal

Mrs. Hildebrand and her third-grade class at Jefferson School, 2008–2009, my helpers, and to their annoying siblings, too

Lauren Rille, Caitlyn Dlouhy, and Ann Bobco, with appreciation

Donald H. McGhee, who bought ice cream sundaes with his hot-lunch money

John Brett, who survived a long winter

And to everybody who finds themselves on these pages!

Here are some of my favorite treats—Try them!

Dessert

LEMON SQUARES

½ cup plus 1 tbsp. butter
1 cup flour
1¼ cup confection. sugar
¼ tsp. salt
1 cup sugar
½ tsp. b. powder
2 eggs
4 tbsp. lemon juice

Mix ½ cup butter, flour ½ cup conf. sugar, 1/8 tsp. salt. Pack in 8 X 8-inch pan. Bake for 15 min. (350) Remove from oven. Combine white sugar, b. powder, remain. salt, eggs, 2 tbsp. lemon juice and spread over baked mixture. Bake 20 min.(350) Cool; spread ~~over baked mixture. B~~ with glaze made of remaining lemon juice, powdered sugar and butter. Yield: 16-20 squares.

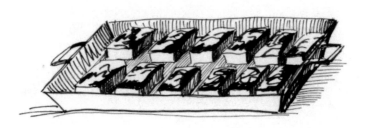

DOUBLE-DECKER CHOCOLATE BARS

2 well-beaten eggs
1 cup sugar
1 cup sifted flour
½ cup chopped pecans
About 1½ sticks butter
2½ 1-oz. squares unsweetened baker's chocolate
2 cups sifted confectionary sugar
2 tbsp. milk
½ tsp. vanilla

Combine first 4 ingredients with ½ cup melted butter and 2 sqs. melted chocolate. Spread in 8" square pan. Bake in 350-degree oven for 20-25 minutes; cool. Combine con. sugar, 2 tbsp. butter, milk and vanilla; spread over baked layer. Chill 10 minutes. Combine remaining choc. and 1½ tsp. butter. Spread or drizzle over top. Cool 30 minutes. Cut into bars. Yield:32 bars

Beggarman's Rice Pudding

Stir frequently

1 can evaporated milk, diluted by one can of
water
1/3-cup rice.
1/8 tsp. salt.
1/4-cup sugar.

Cook all ingredients in top of a double
boiler, no lid, till liquid is absorbed.
(Roughly one hour.) Remove from heat, and add
1/4 tsp. nutmeg, 1/2-cup raisins (soak a bit
first) and 1/2 tsp. vanilla.

then drain

Note: Skin will keep re-absorbing